Includes Compact Disc

John Jacob Jingleheimer Schmidt

Retold by STEVEN ANDERSON
Illustrated by CONNAH BRECON

CANTATA
LEARNING

WWW.CANTATALEARNING.COM

CANTATA
LEARNING

Published by Cantata Learning
1710 Roe Crest Drive
North Mankato, MN 56003
www.cantatalearning.com

Library of Congress Control Number: 2015932823
Anderson, Steven
        John Jacob Jingleheimer Schmidt / retold by Steven Anderson; Illustrated by
Connah Brecon
        Series: Sing-along Silly Songs
        Audience: Ages: 3–8; Grades: PreK–3
        Summary: In this silly song a boy sees his reflection in many places.
        ISBN: 978-1-63290-379-2 (library binding/CD)
        ISBN: 978-1-63290-510-9 (paperback/CD)
        ISBN: 978-1-63290-540-6 (paperback)
        1. Stories in rhyme.

Book design and art direction, Tim Palin Creative
Editorial direction, Flat Sole Studio
Music direction, Elizabeth Draper
Music arranged and produced by Steven C Music

Printed in the United States of America in North Mankato, Minnesota.
122015   0326CGS16

Have you ever met someone with the same name as yours? That is what this song is all about. The first **verse** of "John Jacob Jingleheimer Schmidt" is often sung loudly. Each verse is then sung a little softer, with the last one being just a **whisper**.

Now turn the page and get ready to sing along!

my
name
is
John Jacob
Jingleheimer
my
name
is
John Jacob
Jingleheime

John Jacob Jingleheimer Schmidt,
his name is my name, too.

Whenever we go out,
the people always **shout** and sing.

"John Jacob Jingleheimer Schmidt!"

Da da da da da da da.

John Jacob Jingleheimer Schmidt,
his name is my name, too.

Whenever we go out,
the people always shout and sing.

"John Jacob Jingleheimer Schmidt!"

Da da da da da da da.

John Jacob Jingleheimer Schmidt,
his name is my name, too.

Whenever we go out,
the people always shout and sing.

"John Jacob Jingleheimer Schmidt!"

Da da da da da da da.

John Jacob Jingleheimer Schmidt,
his name is my name, too.

Whenever we go out,
the people always shout and sing.

"John Jacob Jingleheimer Schmidt!"

Da da da da da da da.

SONG LYRICS
John Jacob Jingleheimer Schmidt

John Jacob Jingleheimer Schmidt,
his name is my name, too.

Whenever we go out,
the people always shout and sing.

"John Jacob Jingleheimer Schmidt!"
Da da da da da da da.

John Jacob Jingleheimer Schmidt,
his name is my name, too.

Whenever we go out,
the people always shout and sing.

"John Jacob Jingleheimer Schmidt!"
Da da da da da da da.

John Jacob Jingleheimer Schmidt,
his name is my name, too.

Whenever we go out,
the people always shout and sing.

"John Jacob Jingleheimer Schmidt!"
Da da da da da da da.

John Jacob Jingleheimer Schmidt,
his name is my name, too.

Whenever we go out,
the people always shout and sing.

"John Jacob Jingleheimer Schmidt!"
Da da da da da da da.

John Jacob Jingleheimer Schmidt

Ska
Steven C. Music

GLOSSARY

shout—to call out loudly

verse—one part of a poem or song

whisper—to talk very quietly

GUIDED READING ACTIVITIES

1. The boy in this story keeps seeing his reflection. Where can you see your reflection?

2. Look at the last illustration in this book. Can you tell where the boy is? How does he look? Have you ever seen mirrors like these?

3. How many letters are in "John Jacob Jingleheimer Schmidt"? Write, or have someone help you write, your entire name. How many letters are in your name? Whose name is longer?

TO LEARN MORE

Freeman-Hines, Laura. *Here We Go Looby Loo: Children's Favorite Activity Songs*. Mankato, MN: Child's World, 2011.

Singer, Marilyn. *Follow Follow: A Book of Reverso Poems*. New York: Dial Books for Young Readers, 2013.

Snedeker, Gus. *Campfire Songs, Ballads, and Lullabies: Folk Music*. Broomall, PA: Mason Crest, 2013.

Wood, Hannah. *Old MacDonald Had a Farm: And Other Favorite Children's Songs*. Wilton, CT: Tiger Tales, 2012.